Noir Suspicions

Book by
David Landau

Music and Lyrics by
Nikki Stern

A SAMUEL FRENCH ACTING EDITION

SAMUEL
FRENCH

FOUNDED 1830

SAMUELFRENCH.COM
SAMUELFRENCH-LONDON.CO.UK

FOR PRODUCTION ENQUIRIES

UNITED STATES AND CANADA
Info@SamuelFrench.com
1-866-598-8449

UNITED KINGDOM AND EUROPE
Theatre@SamuelFrench-London.co.uk
020-7255-4302

Each title is subject to availability from Samuel French, depending upon country of performance. Please be aware that *NOIR SUSPICIONS* may not be licensed by Samuel French in your territory. Professional and amateur producers should contact the nearest Samuel French office or licensing partner to verify availability.

MUSIC USE NOTE

Licensees are solely responsible for obtaining formal written permission from copyright owners to use copyrighted music in the performance of this play and are strongly cautioned to do so. If no such permission is obtained by the licensee, then the licensee must use only original music that the licensee owns and controls. Licensees are solely responsible and liable for all music clearances and shall indemnify the copyright owners of the play(s) and their licensing agent, Samuel French, against any costs, expenses, losses and liabilities arising from the use of music by licensees. Please contact the appropriate music licensing authority in your territory for the rights to any incidental music.

IMPORTANT BILLING AND CREDIT REQUIREMENTS

If you have obtained performance rights to this title, please refer to your licensing agreement for important billing and credit requirements.

AUTHOR'S NOTES

I invented the interactive mystery play back in the early 1980s as an attempt to mix environmental theater with audience involvement. My goal was to allow the audience to experience the story as if they were extras in a movie. The entire production, from script to props, direction to surroundings, was oriented towards encompassing the audience in the world of the mystery and not merely with the game of solving it. Mystery parlor games existed since the turn of the century. As theater, it is the story of the characters which must always take center stage - a story of people who find themselves in desperate situations and are compelled to perform desperate acts. The comedy must come from the characters and not at their expense or that of the story.

It can become tempting for cast members to play for a laugh, but this seldom works. The audience laughs the most at things that are played straight - discovering the humor for themselves. Audiences identify and sympathize with characters that are real and seldom with caricatures. An actor's approach to an interactive mystery should be no different than that taken to Shakespeare or any other theatrical work. Why is the character there, what are they thinking, why are they doing what they do and what do they want? The more real, the more the audience becomes involved in this new reality and the more both they and the performers will enjoy the experience. The audience itself is utilized by the performer, as a prop, a confident, another cast member. The audience is on stage with them.

In a true mystery there can be only one logical culprit, pointed out not only by the clues, but by the motivation, personality and situation that character finds himself/herself in. While there are a number of other likely suspects, this character is the inevitable guilty party. The mystery has been sewn well when the average of correct guesses is 10 - 20%. By the end of the play, when all is revealed, the audience should sigh a collective "Of course, I should have thought of that!"

The interactive mystery play offers theater patrons, performers and producers many unique opportunities. The audience can be taken to the edge with suspense and then suddenly dropped into a humorous release of tension. The characters can become so real that they can reach out and touch the audience, literally. The theatrical fourth wall is placed behind the audience. If done correctly, the interactive play can be one of the most involving forms of theater possible.

David Landau
Creator of the first interactive mystery play, "The Mystery Express", Dec. 1982
Member of The Dramatists Guild and Mystery Writers of America

PRODUCTION NOTES

PERFORMANCE SPACE
The following play was designed to be performed in a dining room, dinner theater, night club, theater-in-the-round, or a thrust stage where the acting area is level with the first row. The intention is to make the audience feel like they are actually in the location of the story. The performance is a sort of reverse theater in the round, with action performed around the circumference of the seating area, as well as down the aisles and in the center. The audience should be seated at tables, either dinner or cocktail. Tables could be added in font of the first row in the case of thrust or arena stages. Audience members can also be seated on stage.

SCENES & BREAKS
The script is formatted into four or five scenes running in length from 12 to 20 minutes. Between each scene is time to serve a course of a meal, serve drinks, or play music as desired. During these breaks characters mingle, helping to establish character and reveal information to the audience in a one on one manner. The script can easily be adapted to eliminate some of these breaks. If this is the desire, black-outs should take place between scenes, with an intermission between either scenes 2 and 3 (if four scenes) or 3 and 4 (if five scenes). There should be some kind of break just before the finale scene to allow audience members to hand in their guesses as to "whodunit".

MUSICAL NUMBERS
The musical numbers in the show have been designed to be performed to a taped play back. Once a license has been signed, an

audio tape with recordings of both the instrumentals and the com-
poser singing the lyrics can be obtained from MTG. Lead sheets
will be provided when available. Also in the tape is the opening
theme music which is to be used at the beginning of each scene.
There is a minor fee for the copying and shipping fee of the tape.
For more information contact MTG Inc. via email at
murdertogo@att.net or at (973) 301-0121

AWARDING PRIZES

The "Sleuth Sheets" are handed out with the programs at the beginning of the night and collected by the characters before the finale
scene. They should be handed to the stage manager, who will sort
out the correct answers. After the curtain call, the correct answers
are handed to the main character, who reads out the names of the
successful sleuths. Generally, all correct answers are placed in a
hat and a character draws one name. A prize is then awarded to
that patron by a cast member. The prize can be a bottle of wine, a
T-shirt, almost anything. It's the thought that counts.

CAST

RICHARD ARCHER — ex-private detective, now half owner of the Cafe Noir. His partner and girlfriend is -

SHEILA WONDERLY— ex-call girl, now the other half owner of the Cafe Noir.

ANTHONY CAIRO — a dealer in the black market, and hiding out from some smugglers he double-crossed.

DEPUTY INSPECTOR RIGFIELD — of the St. Vincent Police. He hates the Cafe Noir and has longed to close it down and get himself a promotion to full inspector.

INGRID LASZLO — A desperate woman being blackmailed.

SIDNEY FERRARI — the British owner of the Blue Parrot Resort and Condos on Tobago Cay and one of the Carribean=s wealthiest developers.

CLAUDETTE PONTE — A French blackmailer, known as Nurse Nightshade because of her expertise with poisons.

JUDGE KOCH — (same actress as Claudette) A Magistrate from St. Vincent and regular at the Cafe Noir.

RENAULT — a taxi driver and member of the radical French Liberte party (same actor as Rigfield).

SETTING

The Cafe Noir on the island of Mustique, where everything and everyone is in black, white or grey. Everyone dresses and talks like a character from a 1940s film noir movie. The time, however, is the present. The program looks like a passport to Mustique. Inside is a Sleuth Sheet asking "Whodunit? Whydunit? How many references to the classic movie Casablanca are mentioned during the show?"

As guests enter they are seated by Rick, Sheila and Cairo. Rigfield lurks outside or in the lobby.

A newspaper on every table reads:

"The international French banker, Louis Ugarte was found shot dead on the Kingstown docks last night, a possible robbery victim, as both his wallet and passport were missing. Police are investigating the matter. Mr. Ugarte was staying at the new Blue Parrot Resort on Tobago Cay, which he represented foreign interest in. Tourism fell last year to an all-time low, proving a bust for the new hotel and casinos that recently opened on Tobago Cay. The significant drop in crime last year was looked on as an encouraging sign by the developers, who have said that they're in the Grenadines for the long haul. While some are over-extended, all are competing with each other to develop or at least purchase more property, anticipating the Grenadines as the new vacation center for the international elite. It better come soon, as all the new resort developments have filed for chapter 11."

PRE-SHOW

Rick introduces himself as the manager and owner - co-owner actually, of the Cafe Noir - formerly a Private Investigator from Atlantic City. He invites guests to join the blackjack game in the back room and warns them to stay away from the Blue Parrot resort and Casino, which is a high class rip-off joint. The tables are rigged.

Sheila introduces herself as the manager and owner of the Cafe Noir - co-owner actually. She welcomes them to "her" island and explains that she can help them find anything they may want on the island, from private escorted tours to the best nude beaches. She flirts with the men.

Cairo hands out his business card, which is totally black. He explains that he's a dealer in the blackmarket and has lots of bargains for them. He reveals an arm-full of watches and offers handcuffs and handcuff keys for sale "You never know when they'll come in handy." He tries to sell all sorts of other things (anything the actor wishes to bring in).

Sidney Ferrari introduces himself as a businessman and entrepreneur, handing out business cards. He flirts with the women and tells the men he has some wonderful investment opportunities. Most recently, he is looking to expand his resort properties holdings.

Constable Rigfield walks around, basically accusing people of being criminals and warning them that he is going to close this place down and arrest them all.

Ingrid moves about, wearing sunglasses. She approaches guests, but seems too nervous to say anything and quickly leaves.

Scene 1

(Music plays. A spotlight comes up on RICK as he lights a match. He has a cigarette in his mouth. He lights two candles on a small table as he talks to the audience, with the cigarette still in his mouth.)

RICK. Have you ever wondered if there is any truth to those stupid superstitions? You know, like Friday the thirteenth, breaking a mirror or three on a match?

(He holds up the match ready to light the cigarette, but blows it out instead. He shows that he is wearing handcuffs.)

RICK. The cold steel bracelets of the law. I ended up wearing these because I never believed in superstition. I'm not saying that if I had things would have been different. Although it sure couldn't have been worse. Right know you're probably asking yourself - who the hell is this guy and why on earth is he talking to us. Well, I'm going to tell you, with all the sordid details. My handle is Richard Archer, but you can call me just plain Rick. I'm the

manager of a dark and seedy cafe on the forgotten Caribbean island
of Mustique in the Grenadines. It's a gathering place of sorts,
where all walks of life come together. And that's not always a
good thing. It's a supper club really, called the Cafe Noir.

*(The lights come up over the audience. RICK begins to walk among
     them, pointing people out as he sings. In the shadows are the
     others who sing the chorus.)*

RICK.
HUSTLERS ON HIATUS
TOUGH GUYS OFF THE TAKE
DAMES WHO PAY FOREVER
FOR AN INNOCENT MISTAKE
LIVING IN THE SHADOWS
IT'S THE ONLY LIFE THEY KNOW
DENIZEN OR DROP-OUT
THEY'VE GOT NOWHERE ELSE TO GO

WELCOME TO CAFE NOIR
A CHEAP DOCK-SIDE BAR
POSSESSED OF A QUAINT SEEDY CHARM
MOST OF YOU
WILL BE PASSING ON THROUGH
BUT IF YOU'D LIKE TO STAY
WHAT'S THE HARM
YOU'RE IN CAFE NOIR
AN ALL PURPOSE BAR
WE DON'T CARE WHERE YOU'VE HUNG OUT BEFORE
IF YOUR MONEY'S OKAY
THEN YOU'RE WELCOME TO STAY

WE CAN ALWAYS FIND ROOM FOR ONE MORE.

RICK. My partner in this venture was a an ex-call girl by the name of Sheila Wonderly - a woman who had seen more of the underside of life than _____ *(Whoever is topical.)*

SHEILA. *(Walking about, then joining RICK.)*
EVERY NOW AND THEN
A GROUP OF TOURISTS COME TO CALL
MY, THE PLACE GETS LIVELIER
WITH PARTYING AND ALL
CRAZY FOLKS, THEY DANCE AND DRINK
UNTIL THE BREAK OF DAY
THEN THEY GO
BUT DON'T YOU KNOW, THAT ONE OR TWO MIGHT STAY

RICK & SHEILA.	**CHORUS.**
BECAUSE AT CAFE NOIR	HERE ON THE
THIS FINE ISLAND BAR	ISLAND
WE SERVE PREMIUM CARIBBEAN BOOZE	FINE BOOZE
TOP DRAWER RUM	THIS FINE OLD
IS A DIET FOR SOME	ISLAND
BUT THEN THAT'S THE LIFESTYLE	YOU CHOOSE
THEY CHOOSE	OUT ON THE
YOU SEE, AT CAFE NOIR	ISLAND
YOUR TYPICAL BAR	OOH
WE'RE DESIGNED TO HELP PATRONS FORGET	
IF THE LIQUOR IS SMOOTH	
IT MIGHT HELP TO SOOTH	
ANY LINGERING TRACE OF REGRET	

RICK. You won't find it listed in any of the tourist guides. Our clientele range from the lowest two-bit criminal dining on his last stolen dime to high society dames slumming it with some sap with a seeping wallet. It's a safe haven for people in high-risk professions, where every shadow is a place of business and every transaction is non-refundable. It's the kind of place the British minority government is not really fond of - they say its bad for the island's image. But I run a strictly honest joint and don't take a cut from any of the merchants that use my place to hang their shingle. That's why the bobbies here haven't been able to clamp down and nail this place shut. That is, until - But I'm getting ahead of myself.

RICK & SHEILA.
ANSWERING TO NO ONE
MAKING OUR OWN RULES
FREE TO CUT OUR LOSSES
AND TO WALK AWAY FROM FOOLS
DON'T MEAN TO SOUND CYNICAL
BUT HEY, THAT'S HOW WE SOUND
THE SETUP'S WORKING WELL FOR US
AND THIS IS WHAT WE'VE FOUND

CHORUS.

AT CAFE NOIR — LIFE ON THE
JUST A CHEAP DOCKSIDE BAR — DOCKSIDE
NO ONE CARES WHAT YOU'VE DONE
OR WHO YOU ARE — SO FAR
YOU CAN COME YOU CAN GO
AND THERE'S ALWAYS THE SHOW
THAT PLAY'S OUT EVERY NIGHT AT THE BAR — CAFE
YOU CAN DISAPPEAR — NOIR
YOU CAN TOSS BACK YOUR BEER

IT'S WHATEVER YOU WANT IT TO BE   OOH
CAUSE WE OWN THIS SPACE
AND IN THIS KIND OF PLACE
THERE'S AN ODD SENSE OF BEING FREE   WE'RE FREE

ALL.
THAT'S WHY CAFE NOIR
IS THE PERFECT HOME FOR ME.

(Lights dim to only spotlight on RICK. CLAUDETTE, INGRID, SIDNEY and RIGFIELD exit.)

RICK. The reason I'm bending your ear is because I'm going to ask for your help to get me out of these (holds up handcuffed wrists). But let's start off at an easy place, at a time earlier tonight when I was wearing the same accessories as I'm wearing now, only under different circumstances.

(Lights up. CAIRO approaches, dangling a handcuff key.)

CAIRO. These are the exact same model that the St. Vincent Police department are issued. Now you might see why owning your very own key could be a possession one finds handy.
RICK. For you, certainly, Mr. Cairo. But I'm strictly on the up and up and they know it. That's why they hate me so much. I'm afraid I'm not buying, so if you don't mind?

(RICK holds forward his handcuffed hands for CAIRO to unlock. CAIRO reluctantly starts to, but SHEILA swipes the key and hides it behind her back.)

SHEILA. What's your hurry, big boy? Maybe we should go into the back room and try some new interrogation procedures.

(SHEILA starts to back up as RICK moves after her for the key.)

CAIRO. Of course, if it's the complete set you wish to procure, I could see fit to let you have it for a reasonable sum. Like I did for this couple over here. *(To couple in audience.)* That leather strapped chair and whip will be in by the end of the week.

(RICK loops his arms over SHEILA and kisses her. When he lifts his arms back again, he has the key swiped from her hand behind her back during the kiss and unlocks himself.)

SHEILA. Cheat.

RICK. *(Handing back handcuffs and key.)* Here you go, Cairo. I don't think I'll be in any need of them.

CAIRO. *(Taking handcuffs and keys.)* One can never be too sure. Look how handy the key came in already.

(An ear-shattering whistle sounds and RIGFIELD enters. CAIRO quickly hides the handcuffs and key and starts to slowly back out.)

SHEILA. *(Putting on British accent.)* Evening Deputy Inspector Rigfield. A spot of tea?

RIGFIELD. I'm on duty in my official capacity, Ms. Wonderly.

RICK. What is it this time, Rigfield? Noise complaint? Someone didn't get the right change?

RIGFIELD. A missing shipment of new handcuffs bound for

the St. Vincent's police department. Seems the shackles got snatched last night while the shoreman were distracted in a shell game. When the constable assigned to escort the shipment did his duty and broke up the scam, the damn darbies disappeared from the dock.

RICK. That still doesn't explain why you're showing your face here. It's bad for business. Ruins our customers' appetites.

RIGFIELD. Think you're funny, don't ya, Yank! Well, I distinctly recall seeing someone resembling a friend of yours lurking about the docks last night and I knew I could corner him here. Mr. Cairo!

(RIGFIELD turns to stare down CAIRO.)

CAIRO. You weren't that unfortunate assigned constable that had such an important shipment stolen from right under his very nose? How humiliating. And I had so much faith in you, Deputy Inspector. *(To audience member.)* Constables aren't what they used to be, are they?

(RIGFIELD approaches the same audience member.)

RIGFIELD. *(To audience member.)* You? Out on bail already? The system isn't what it used to be either if it's letting the likes of you walk so fast.

(CAIRO has taken the opportunity to drop the handcuffs into his pocket.)

CAIRO. Perhaps the system didn't let him/her out. Perhaps he/she let him/herself out and it would be your sworn duty to put him back in.

RIGFIELD. Oh, you'd like that, wouldn't you, Mr. Cairo? Run this bloke in while you take a run yourself, aye? Dream on. I'm running you both in.

(RIGFIELD handcuffs CAIRO and then handcuffs him to the audience member.)

RICK. You'd better have an arrest warrant, Rigfield. Otherwise the only uniform you'll be wearing will be as a doorman for the new casino hotel over on Tobago Cay.

RIGFIELD. *(Turning back on CAIRO.)* Think you're smart, aye, peeper? We'll see who's smart when I put you away for aiding and abetting a gunsel.

RICK & SHEILA. Gunsel?

(SHEILA and RICK look at each other, confused. Meanwhile, CAIRO has been removing the handcuffs with his key. CAIRO seats the guests and follows RIGFIELD as he walks towards RICK.)

RIGFIELD. Murderer! That shipment of handcuffs wasn't the only thing that got swiped dockside last night. *(Walking towards RICK, with CAIRO directly behind him.)* Some wealthy off-islander had his life swiped from him as well. Seems the poor bloke was just out for a night stroll and got walked all over. The odd thing was, he had his wallet and everything still on him. What's the matter, peeper? Forgot to read today's paper?

RICK. I haven't had time. And you should know by now, Rigfield, I'm no longer a private detective.

RIGFIELD. That's a laugh - ha, ha. A guy like you can't help it. It's in your blood. Once a dick, always a dick.

SHEILA. Can I quote you on that one, Deputy Inspector?

RIGFIELD. What? *(Realizing what he just said.)* Oh - er - certainly not.

RICK. And what in that confused mind of yours brings me into this little picture?

RIGFIELD. This!

(RIGFIELD pulls out a "Cafe Noir" matchbook.)

RIGFIELD. "Cafe Noir - exquisite island ambiance". It was found at the scene of the crime.

CAIRO. *(Taking matchbook from RIGFIELD.)* I'm disappointed in you, Mr. Rick. After all the business we've done together, to find that you've gone to someone else for something as simple as matchbooks - *(Feels the cover.)* - And even a lower quality than I would have gotten you. I'm sure I could have gotten this for you at half the price you paid. What price did you pay?

RIGFIELD. *(Swiping back the matchbook.)* That's police property - possible evidence at a probable homicide.

SHEILA. It's just a matchbook with "Cafe Noir" printed on it. Anyone could have picked one up.

RIGFIELD. But I don't see any on the tables, Miss Wonderly. Do you?

(She and CAIRO look around. There are no matchbooks out.)

RICK. Rest assured, Cairo, if ever I had matchbooks for this place printed up, I'd do them through you. But that's one thing I've never gotten around to.

CAIRO. Then how do you explain that?

RIGFIELD. Precisely!

RICK. I'm afraid I can't.

RIGFIELD. Right! Keep a lid on it as long as you can, peeper. But I'll have it all out. And when I do, I'll have you right where I want you, in St. Vincent's prison.

(RIGFIELD turns and starts to leave. CAIRO hands him his handcuffs as he passes. RIGFIELD just nods in thanks, then finally stops by the door.)

RIGFIELD. Wait one bloody second. How did you get out of these here darbies?

CAIRO. I didn't.

RIGFIELD. You can't play me for a sap, sharpie. I don't see your wrists still in them, do I?

CAIRO. Very funny, Deputy Inspector. You let me out, when Mr. Rick asked if you had an arrest warrant. *(To audience member he was handcuffed to.)* He's always one for a good gag, isn't he, the deputy inspector here? *(To RIGFIELD.)* You're a sharp one, sir, there's no denying that.

RIGFIELD. You can bet your cards on it. *(To RICK.)* I'm watching you, Archer. You're going to feel my eyes pressing in on your back so hard you're not going to be able to sleep at night.

(RIGFIELD exits.)

SHEILA. I knew we shouldn't have stayed open for Friday the 13th.

CAIRO. That's right! This is Friday the 13th. If I were you, Mr. Rick, I'd close up fast.

RICK. Close up? We've got a fine crowd here tonight.

(SHEILA, CAIRO and RICK look about at the crowd. There is dis-
appointment and disgust on their faces.)

ALL THREE. Ugh.

RICK. Okay, maybe not so fine a crowd. But superstition is
just that and it doesn't pay the bills.

SHEILA. No? Everyone knows that you knock on wood
after mentioning your own good fortune. Right? Just a silly superstition. *(Walking to a man in the audience.)* Well, just the other day
this fine gentleman found himself before a St. Vincent Magistrate
after being arrested for swindling a couple of vacationing nuns. He
played poker with the judge to determine his sentencing. When our
friend had three duces in his hand, he knocked on the wooden table
the cards were dealt on. The table collapsed and in the confusion
he picked up two of a kind from a previous hand. His newly con-
structed full house easily beat the judge's three jacks - and that's
how he ended up here instead of in a St. Vincent's jail cell.

CAIRO. You might say he played his cards right when
opportunity knocked. And what of spilled salt? A supposed warning of impending danger that could only be offset by the tossing of
some grains over one's left shoulder - to blind the devil lurking
there. Superstition, without doubt. *(Walking up to a woman.)* But
when this wonderful specimen of womanhood had completed her
work at the Grenadine Hyatt last night, she stumbled into a tray of
room service in the hall. She might never have been able to be with
us tonight, if she had not thrown the spilled salt over her left shoulder, thus blinding the hotel detective about to apprehend her for
prostitution. Excellent service at reasonable rates - my personal
recommendation.

SHEILA. I gave her all my old clients. You know, Rick, this
is one of those rare occasions when I actually agree with Cairo. We

shouldn't have opened tonight and I think we should close up early before any more harm is done.

RICK. This is ludicrous! If I'm not going to close up under threat of the St. Vincent police, I'm certainly not going to close for a silly superstition.

(CAIRO, sensing the tension, backs into the shadows.)

SHEILA. *(Angry)* You? I'm the co-manager of Cafe Noir, aren't I?

RICK. Well -

SHEILA. Well, this 50% says we close and cut our losses before they cut us.

RICK. Alright, I'll keep my half of the place open and you can close your 50%. *(Pointing to a few tables.)* You can have that half. But I'd be pretty careful about how you ask them to leave. Some of them look pretty scary.

(INGRID, wearing sunglasses, enters.)

SHEILA. We're closed.

(She turns and starts to exit.)

RICK. We're open.

(She turns and starts back in.)

SHEILA. *(Angry look to RICK.)* WE'RE CLOSED!

(She turns and starts to exit.)

RICK. This half of the place is open.

(She turns back and starts in again.)

SHEILA. But she's in my half so we're closed.

(INGRID looks totally confused.)

INGRID. Well, it doesn't really matter much to me either way. I didn't come here for dinner or a drink. I was looking for a gentleman by the name of Richard Archer.
RICK. You just found him.
SHEILA. And you can keep him.

(SHEILA storms out. RICK starts after her.)

INGRID. I hope this isn't an awkward moment.
RICK. *(Giving up on SHEILA.)* No more awkward than any other. My life seems to be just one awkward moment after another. What can I do for you, Ms.?
INGRID. *(Covers her left hand with her right.)* Ingrid. I've heard you are a man who can be trusted.
RICK. It's nice to hear someone disagrees with the loan officer at my bank. Go on.
INGRID. Well, it's a delicate matter, one that requires a certain amount of discretion.
RICK. In other words, you don't want your husband to find out.
INGRID. What makes you think I have a husband to find out?
RICK. The way you hid your left hand when I asked your

name. You should have taken the wedding ring off before you came in the door. I'm sure whoever gave you my name told you I used to be a private detective.

INGRID. Yes, of course. That is why I came here.

RICK. But they forgot to tell you that I quit that occupation. I didn't like the hours or the working conditions and most of the time they didn't like me. I'm the manager, co-manager actually, of this little supper club now. Don't take this the wrong way, Ms. Ingrid, I'm flattered that you would come to me for help. But unless it's a drink or something to eat, I'm afraid the only way I can help you out is the same way you came in.

INGRID. *(Holding back the upset in her voice.)* I see. Well, I'm sorry if I've wasted any of your time. Good evening then, Mr. Archer.

(She turns to leave and suddenly breaks down crying. RICK turns to the audience. Ingrid freezes.)

RICK. Okay folks, if you were in my shoes, what would you have done? I could hear her sob story or just help her get a taxi back to her hotel. With a show of hands, how many for taking it on the chin and helping Ingrid with her problem?

(RICK counts the votes.)

RICK. Okay, and how many for keeping my nose clean and helping her out - the door, that is?

(RICK counts the votes. Scene continues with version A or B.)

VERSION - A "To Help"

If the majority voted to help her out, Rick replies;

RICK. A bunch of saps here tonight, falling for the old waterworks routine, huh! Alright, majority rules.

(RICK comforts her and hands her his hanky.)

RICK. That's alright, Sister. Have a good cry and then tell me all about it. I've always had a weakness for Niagra Falls. Let me get you a drink on the house while we wait for the flood gates to close.

(RICK turns to leave for the bar. Skip to "Both Versions Continue.")

VERSION - B "Not to Help"

If the majority voted to send her back to her hotel, RICK replies:

RICK. Heartless bunch here tonight, not even touched by the old waterworks routine, huh? Alright, majority rules.

(RICK comforts her and hands her his hanky.)

RICK. That's alright, Sister. Have a good cry and you'll discover that things aren't really all that bad. Go back to your hotel and then, if you still feel desperate come morning, you can give me a call. Let me get you a drink on the house and I'll put in a call for a taxi.

(RICK hands her his card. He turns to leave for the bar.)

BOTH VERSIONS CONTINUE

INGRID. Thank you, Mr. Archer.

RICK. That's just plain Rick.

INGRID. Very well then. Thank you Mr. just plain Rick.

(CAIRO steps forward intercepting RICK.)

CAIRO. There is something very familiar about that woman, Mr. Rick. Something that gives me a very uneasy feeling.

RICK. Well, she's a new face to me, Cairo.

CAIRO. *(Feeling scars on his face.)* Just because a face is new, it doesn't mean it's innocent.

RICK. Speaking as one who knows?

CAIRO. In more ways than one, Mr. Rick. Yes, in more ways than one. The sooner you have her out of here the better for us all.

RICK. And what superstition is it this time?

CAIRO. The seven years bad luck one.

(CAIRO points to INGRID, who has opened a compact mirror to adjust her make-up. The mirror is cracked.)

RICK. Maybe she's had that cracked make-up mirror for seven years already. Maybe you could sell her a new one?

(RICK goes to the bar and gets a drink. As INGRID adjusts her make-up, she notices in the mirror CLAUDETTE, wearing sunglasses and a dark hat, enter. She becomes nervous and closes the compact quickly. CAIRO approaches INGRID as CLAUDETTE fades back into the shadows, watching INGRID.)

CAIRO. Pardon me, Madam. But I couldn't help noticing that your make-up mirror is in a damaged condition.

INGRID. Yes, it seems to have broken on my way over here this evening. Bad luck, aye?

(RICK has returned with her drink in time to hear this. CAIRO shoots him an "I told you so" glance.)

CAIRO. Perhaps your luck can be changed.

(CAIRO opens his jacket to display a variety of compacts. INGRID laughs. CAIRO looks offended and starts away.)

RICK. Thank you, Mr. Cairo. You've changed her from tears to laughter. And such a beautiful laugh it is.

(RICK hands her the drink. Continue with either Version A or skip to Version B as marked.)

VERSION - A "To Help"

RICK. Okay, Sister, let's have it. What problem is it you'd like me to help you with that you can't go to the police about?

INGRID. You say you are no longer a private detective, but you still talk like one.

RICK. Hard habits are bad to break. What are you being blackmailed for?

INGRID. *(Surprised)* But - who said anything about black-mail?

RICK. Let's get something straight between us, Ingrid. You came here for my help and against my better judgement I'm throwing in with you. But my help comes with certain conditions - no games, no lies. Neither of us have time for it. What are you being blackmailed over? Photos?

INGRID. A pearl necklace. It was a gift from a certain friend.

RICK. A lover.

(She looks at him, cross.)

RICK. Well, if you can't stick to the rules, there's no sense in playing the game.

(RICK turns and starts away.)

INGRID. Alright, yes, a lover. We met in Paris. When my husband went to Germany on business, we spent the week in Casablanca, where he bought me a set of perfectly shaped pearls from some dealer in the black-market. The pearls were held together by a locket which had a dedication inside.

RICK. Could be from childhood sweetheart days. Not substantial enough for a good ransom.

INGRID. The dedication was dated.

RICK. That's substantial enough. Your husband is a jealous man?

INGRID. Violently. As a boy every time his dog gave the stick to someone else to throw, he beat it.

RICK. So this wouldn't just be to protect your lover, but yourself as well.

INGRID. I suppose that's true.

RICK. And your husband is rich and you're accustomed to being pampered.

INGRID. I'm not sure I like your directness, just plain Rick.

RICK. That's your choice, I guess.

INGRID. *(Handing RICK a stuffed gray envelope.)* I want you to get that necklace and destroy it. There's plenty in there to cover your time and all expenses.

RICK. *(Glancing inside at all $100 bills.)* And where would I find this blackmailer of yours?

INGRID. She's less than twenty feet away. That dangerous looking woman over there.

RICK. *(Pointing to a woman in audience.)* Who, her?

INGRID. No, not her. She's pretty scary, though. But, that woman over there in the black hat and sunglasses.

(INGRID motions towards CLAUDETTE, sipping a drink in the shadows.)

INGRID. I would appreciate it if you would wait until after I've left.

RICK. I have all night.

Skip to "Either Version Continues"

VERSION - B "Not to Help"

RICK. That cab will be a little late. It seems to be a busy night.

Skip to "Either Version Continues"

EITHER VERSION CONTINUES

INGRID. I'm afraid my husband may have followed me. If he caught me here it would put me in a rather awkward position.

RICK. You're more than welcome to wait in the back room.

(RICK motions off to the back room.)

INGRID. Thank you, just plain Rick.

(She gives him a quick kiss, catching RICK off guard, then exits past SHEILA, who has entered and seen this. CAIRO clears his throat as a way to warn RICK.)

   CAIRO. Isn't it time for the first course?

(SHEILA claps her hands, glaring at RICK. The first course is served during which SHEILA goes from table to table asking about the strange woman - what's her name, what did she want, how was RICK acting towards her. SHEILA seems jealous. SHEILA tells guests that she can recommend some rather good escorts on the island, if they are so inclined.

CAIRO moves from table to table trying to sell things and reminding people that he certainly didn't have anything to do with that unfortunate man's death last night down by the docks. Yes, he was down in the area, collecting a shipment, and come to think of it, the description of the man does fit a gentleman CAIRO remembers seeing talking in the shadows with a woman in a trenchcoat, sunglasses, and her hair pulled up into a black hat.

INGRID moves around from table to table, making nervous small talk and obviously trying to avoid CLAUDETTE. If asked by guests what she wanted to hire RICK to do for her, she will reveal that she needs to have something she lost retrieved. She will notice the newspaper on each table, read a portion of it and become obviously upset and put it down again. She knew the man killed on the docks.

CLAUDETTE follows one table behind INGRID, saying good evening to guests and asking what Ingrid has told anyone. If questioned, CLAUDETTE reveals that she has some business with Ingrid and it was INGRID who picked the Cafe Noir as the place to meet and settle the business.

*RICK goes from table to table, welcoming them to Cafe Noir and
    the island of Mustique. He mentions that SHEILA is his part-
    ner and girlfriend, so please don't say anything to her about
    INGRID - as SHEILA is the jealous type. He tries to get a con-
    sensus of guests to agree with him that there's nothing to these
    silly superstitions.*
*RENAULT begins to circulate flyers to each table that declare that
    LOUIS UGARTE was murdered by the British Government of
    St. Vincent because of his connections with the French Liberte
    Party and their never-ending fight for French ex-patriot rule
    of the islands stolen by Imperial Britain [Grenada, St. Lucia,
    St. Kitts & Nevis and St. Vincent & the Grenadines]. The flyer
    calls for the overthrow of the British minority government of
    St. Vincent in favor of a socialist democracy. RENAULT is a
    member and imparts his conviction that the islands are being
    destroyed by too much commercialization and the sale of
    property to foreigners.)*

NOIR SUSPICIONS

Scene 2

(Music intro. SHEILA approaches RICK.)

SHEILA. No wonder you didn't want to close up earlier tonight.

RICK. Maybe you and Cairo are right. This Friday the 13th is turning unlucky.

SHEILA. Because you got caught?

RICK. I didn't do anything to get caught at, Sheila.

SHEILA. Then why did you send little miss lipstick tester to the back room?

RICK. She's just waiting for a taxi to take her back to her hotel and is afraid her husband may have followed her here.

(SHEILA starts to get angry.)

RICK. She wanted to hire me to do some private eye work. I told her I was no longer in the business.

SHEILA. In other words, you told her you were no longer a private dick.

(SIDNEY, in a sports jacket and ascot, enters. SHEILA sees him, smiles at RICK and approaches him.)

SHEILA. *(Sexy)* Evening, stranger. You're a new face. The name's Sheila, Sheila Wonderly, I'm the night manager here. If there's anything I can do for you -

SIDNEY. You've already done it. And I'd say no man would prefer his nights managed by anyone else. The name is Sidney, Sidney Ferrari.

SHEILA. Fast and sleek just like the car, I'll bet.

SIDNEY. I'd be happy to take you for a test drive, Ms. Wonderly. May I call you Sheila?

SHEILA. As often as you like.

SIDNEY. You've never heard of me?

SHEILA. Should I?

SIDNEY. I'm only the wealthiest real estate developer around. Hotels, condos, casinos - I erected that new luxury resort and condo complex on Tobago Cay - the Blue Parrot.

SHEILA. Really? That's quite an erection, Mr Ferrari.

SIDNEY. So you have heard of me?

SHEILA. Nope. Sorry.

SIDNEY. Well, you have a nice spot here. A very a fine location.

(RICK interrupts.)

RICK. You're wasting your time, Mister.

SHEILA. Beat it, Rick. *(To SIDNEY.)* You'll have to excuse my co-manager. He's only jealous because you're rich, handsome and interested.

RICK. Interested in buying this place and tearing it down. Isn't that right, Ferrari?

SIDNEY. Mr. Ferrari to you, Mr - ?

SHEILA & RICK. Just plain Rick.

SIDNEY. Mr. Just Plain Rick.

RICK. Go on. Tell her.

SIDNEY. Tobago Cay has suddenly become the new Mecca for the worldly rich. And all us rich folk do like to slum it at times, for the excitement, you see. A place here on Mustique, a place of style and class catering to a glamorous and *(Looking around audience.)* much more sophisticated clientele, could be tremendously profitable. Some substantial changes would be required, more befitting the clientele and a night manager like yourself.

(He kisses SHEILA'S hand.)

RICK. Cafe Noir is not for sale.

SIDNEY. That would depend on who owns it. And from the records filed in St. Vincent the Cafe Noir is owned jointly by a Mr. Richard Archer and Ms. Sheila Wonderly.

SHEILA. We pooled both our savings and bought it when the place went up for probate after the murder of its first owner a year ago. But that's a different story.

SIDNEY. Maybe you could tell it to me - over dinner tonight on my yacht? I'm sure your assistant manager could handle the place for a night without you.

SHEILA. A tempting offer.

SIDNEY. I can promise you a few more tempting offers to come. I'll get a drink from the bar while you think it over.

(SIDNEY exits to bar.)

RICK. I thought we had something special here. Something dependable that would withstand time and change.

SHEILA. Yeah, so did I.

(CAIRO enters. He seems worried.)

CAIRO. There is a woman here, Ms. Wonderly, that I don't think either of us are particularly delighted to see again. A Mademoiselle Claudette Ponte.

(CAIRO points out CLAUDETTE. CLAUDETTE raises her glass to them. SHEILA becomes very uneasy.)

SHEILA. *(To RICK.)* This is all your fault. You wanted to stay open tonight.

(SHEILA storms away toward the back room. RICK is confused. He looks at the audience. CAIRO turns to leave, but RICK grabs his arm.)

RICK. Who is Claudette Ponte?
CAIRO. That woman over there. I thought I made that fairly obvious.

(CAIRO turns to leave again, and RICK stops him again.)

RICK. That doesn't quite answer my question, Cairo.
CAIRO. Isn't that Miss Ingrid in the back office, where Ms. Wonderly seems to be headed?

(RICK releases CAIRO and dashes out after SHEILA. CLAUDETTE laughs and walks up to CAIRO. RICK stops at the doorway and watches.)

CLAUDETTE. You do know how to empty a room, don't you, Anthony?

CAIRO. Unfortunately, like fine coffee, there always seems to be some dregs left behind.

CLAUDETTE. Your usual quickness. I guess the true test is how quickly you can help me forget something I remember that you'd rather were forgotten.

CAIRO. I can't remember what.

CLAUDETTE. *(To audience member.)* Isn't Cairo cute? That's exactly what I thought to myself as I finished cleaning the instruments after you finished the plastic surgery. I thought to myself how much cuter his entirely new face was compared to the face that had first gone under the knife - the one that was running not just from the law but some even more dangerous adversaries. You, Doctor, probably don't even remember what Mr. Cairo looked like before you started the operation. After all, you were rip-roaring drunk as usual. And to think they took away your license in the States for that. They're so picky, aren't they?

CAIRO. You certainly don't believe a man on the lam would be fool enough to give anyone his real name? Especially to the disbarred doctor and nurse he paid to give him a new identity?

CLAUDETTE. But a face can always be matched with a name, Anthony, or should I say - Johnny? *(Imitating music sting.)* Dun, dun dun!

(CAIRO suddenly shivers. CLAUDETTE laughs. He gives CLAUDETTE a cold, mean glare.)

CAIRO. It is widely agreed that an absence of memory is preferable to an absence of entirety.

CLAUDETTE. As I say to all my "clients" - pay me, or kill me, but don't waste either of our times on threats. Why don't I freshen up my drink while you think the choices over.

(They start to part, when INGRID, followed by an angry SHEILA, comes out from the back room. CLAUDETTE calls out to SHEILA.)

CLAUDETTE. Sheila? Why we haven't seen each other since - last night.

(Everyone stops and looks at CLAUDETTE. SHEILA looks around to see that everyone, including SIDNEY, is listening.)

SHEILA. I haven't the foggiest idea what you're talking about.

(CLAUDETTE places down her drink on a small table and walks up close to SHEILA.)

CLAUDETTE. It was foggy down on the docks, alright. But then again, that is why you went down there with your gentleman friend, isn't it, Ms. Wonder-lay?

(SHEILA looks quickly at RICK then gives CLAUDETTE a cold, menacing glare. CLAUDETTE turns to the audience.)

CLAUDETTE. We were both nursing students in Grenada together some years back. Sheila decided to specialize in, shall we say, nursing male frustration. She made her own work study program.

SHEILA. And you went into toxicology, with a deadly dedication. Peasants came from all over the island to find Nurse Nightshade and pay her for a prescription that would help them bury their problems.

CLAUDETTE. Just as businessmen came to hire the servic-
es of Nurse Feelgood. We both found our special callings in life.

SHEILA. I'm no longer in that line of business, Claudette.
I'm the manager of this supper club now. And what are you doing
here? I hope you're not looking for a bartending job.

CLAUDETTE. *(Short laugh.)* I'm in private enterprise. I
heard this was a good place to transact a little business. Imagine
my pleasant surprise when I noticed Mr. Cairo here and then you.

SHEILA. If you noticed me down on the docks last night,
then you were there too.

CLAUDETTE. Exactly my point. I'm like a stray cat who
quietly watches everything from the shadows. I'm sure we might
see things eye to eye.

*(CLAUDETTE puts down her drink as RENAULT enters, wearing
    a cap and a black arm band.)*

RENAULT. *(French accent.)* Taxi? Someone here require a
cab?

*(CAIRO, SHEILA, SIDNEY and INGRID eagerly say "yes."
    CLAUDETTE laughs. Everyone freezes in place. RICK
    addresses the audience.)*

RICK. Are you lost? I know I was. Everything was coming
in from so many directions, it was as bad as a New Jersey traffic
circle. I was more confused than the time I fell asleep at a double
feature and woke up in the middle of "The Big Sleep." It was like
all the works of Raymond Chandler or Dashell Hammett had
somehow spilled over in my lap and the pages had gotten mixed
together. And here I was, standing in for Humphrey Bogart, but no

one had bothered to give me a copy of the script. There was a corpse on the dock, a mysterious woman, a French blackmailer and a suitor after both my cafe and my femme fatale. Fear seemed to be the biggest customer at Cafe Noir that night. And it was the one customer I reserved the right not to serve.

(RICK picks up CLAUDETTE'S drink and forces it into her hands. Everyone comes back to life.)

RICK. This lady will take your cab, Renault, after she finishes her drink. *(To CLAUDETTE.)* As a matter of fact, you can take the glass with you and finish it on your ride back to whatever rock you crawled out from under.

CLAUDETTE. But I like this rock better. The snakes are so much more familiar.

RICK. Then why don't you come back tomorrow night? I'll save some dead rodents for you. But right now, I've got my own rats and weasels that need some attending to.

CLAUDETTE. I think you're a man I'm going to enjoy doing business with. Cheers!

(She downs the entire drink and hands the glass back to RICK.)

CLAUDETTE. Come on, Renault.This python's had enough charming for one night.

(RENAULT motions for her to go first. As she passes him, she becomes dizzy and collapses into RENAULT'S arms.)

RENAULT. I am a cab driver, mademoiselle. Not a gigolo.

(Music begins as CLAUDETTE sings "Was It -".)

CLAUDETTE.
SOMETHING WAS SLIPPED IN MY DRINK!

    RICK. What?

CLAUDETTE.
SOME SORT OF POISON I THINK.

    CAIRO. How terrible.

CLAUDETTE.
WHAT KIND OF POTION WAS FORCE-FED TO ME?
WHAT KIND OF DEATH AWAITS ME?
"Wait"

MY VISION IS BLURRED
AND I'M DIZZY AS WELL
I'M NAUSEOUS, IT SEEMS
THOUGH IT'S SO HARD TO TELL
WAS IT HEMLOCK OR FOXGLOVE
OR JIMSONWEED PLANT
WAS IT CAMAS OR BANEBERRY
NO, BUT IT CAN'T BE
THERE'RE SO MANY CHOICES
AND SO LITTLE TIME
WHAT WAS IT WAS USED
FOR THIS DEVIOUS CRIME

    INGRID. How awful.

CLAUDETTE.
I'VE GASTRIC DISTRESS
BURNING PAIN IN MY HAND
MY LEGS ARE SO COLD
AND I CAN'T SEEM TO STAND
WAS IT GARLIC I SMELLED
THEN IT'S ARSENIC FOR SURE
WAS THE SCENT YELLOW JASMINE
HOW PLEASANT
"No cure"
WAS IT BETELNUT, BLOODROOT
THE LIST IS SO LONG
WHY NOT HAZARD A GUESS
SO WHAT IF I'M WRONG

SIDNEY. Isn't there anything we can do?

CLAUDETTE.
WAS IT BELLADONNA
THE DREADED DEADLY NIGHTSHADE
THAT WOULD EXPLAIN THE FEVER
AND WHY MY EARS ARE RINGING
PERHAPS I'VE TAKEN MANDRAKE
OR WAS IT OLEANDER
BUT THAT ONE WORKS TOO QUICKLY
AND HERE I AM STILL SINGING
BITTER ALMONDS
DO I TASTE BITTER ALMONDS
THEN WAS IT CYANIDE
UNLESS I'M TASTING RADISH
IN WHICH CASE, WAS IT MONKSHOOD

WHICH GIVES ME SEVERAL MINUTES
AND WILL THEY TRACE IT?

ALL.
NEVER

CLAUDETTE.
WHATEVER IT MIGHT BE
IT MEANS THE END OF ME
"Wait"

THE NUMBNESS SETS IN
NOW THE BREATHING IS TIGHT
I'LL IDENTIFY THE POISON
IF IT TAKES ME ALL NIGHT

(Everyone groans.)

WAS IT STRYCHNINE OR MISTLETOE
BARBADOS NUT
DID THE RAT GIVE ME THALLIUM
"Pain in my gut"
WAS IT BLACK LOCUST WEED
THAT DECIDED MY FATE
I WOULD WELCOME SUGGESTIONS
ALTHOUGH IT WOULD SEEM
IT'S A BIT TOO LATE

(CLAUDETTE dies.)

SHEILA. *(To RICK.)* Perhaps you're right, Rick. Maybe this

isn't an unlucky day after all. Renault, Mr. Cairo, perhaps you could help escort our dear Ms. Ponte to the back room!

RENAULT. But Mademoiselle, *(Loud whisper.)* she is dead!

CAIRO. *(Moving towards the door.)* How astute of you to notice Renault.

SIDNEY. Perhaps Ms. Wonderly feels that a corpse in the dining room might not lend the most appetizing atmosphere.

RENAULT. Ah, oui.

(CAIRO is at the edge of the door.)

CAIRO. 'Love to pitch in, but an urgent business opportunity calls.

(CAIRO dashes out.)

SHEILA. Perhaps, Mr. Ferrari, you might volunteer to assist?

SIDNEY. *(Short laugh.)* Me? I beg your pardon?

SHEILA. Why don't we save the begging for the boudoir?

(SIDNEY smiles and quickly goes to help RENAULT lift CLAUDETTE. SIDNEY and INGRID'S eyes meet for a moment. SHEILA leads the way as SIDNEY and RENAULT follow with CLAUDETTE. INGRID starts to exit.)

RICK. Not so fast, sister.

INGRID. I would hope any affection you might have for me would be anything but sisterly?

RICK. Seems to me you're the one bringing in all this bad luck tonight.

INGRID. I'm afraid it just seems to follow me, like a stray dog - with rabies.

(Scene continues according to vote. If Version A "To Help," skip to marked "Either Version Continues." If Version B "Not to Help," continue here. This is the same mini-scene that would have been skipped previously.)

VERSION - B "Not to Help"

RICK. Okay, Sister, let's have it. What problem was it you'd like me to help you with that you can't go to the police about?

INGRID. You say you are no longer a private eye, but you still talk like one.

RICK. Hard habits are bad to break. What are you being blackmailed for?

INGRID. *(Surprised)* But - who said anything about blackmail?

RICK. Let's get something straight between us, Ingrid. You came here for my help and against my better judgement I'm throwing in with you. But my help comes with certain conditions - no games, no lies. Neither of us have time for it. What are you being blackmailed over? Photos?

INGRID. A pearl necklace. It was a gift from a certain friend.

RICK. A lover.

(She looks at him, cross.)

RICK. Well, if you can't stick to the rules, there's no sense in playing the game.

(He starts to leave.)

INGRID. Alright, yes, a lover. We met in Paris. When my husband went to Germany on business, we spent the week in Casablanca, where he bought me a set of perfectly shaped pearls from some dealer in the black market. The pearls were held together by a locket which had a dedication inside.

RICK. Could be from childhood sweetheart days. Not substantial enough for a good ransom.

INGRID. The dedication was dated.

RICK. That's substantial enough. Your husband is a jealous man?

INGRID. Violently. As a boy every time his dog gave the stick to someone else to throw, he'd beat it.

RICK. So this wouldn't just be to protect your lover, but yourself as well.

INGRID. I suppose that's true.

RICK. And your husband is rich and you're accustomed to being pampered.

INGRID. I'm not sure I like your directness, just plain Rick.

RICK. That's your choice, I guess.

INGRID. *(Handing RICK a stuffed gray envelope.)* I want you to get that necklace and destroy it. There's plenty in there to cover your time and all expenses.

RICK. *(Glancing inside at all $100 bills.)* And where would I find this blackmailer of yours?

INGRID. She's not more than twenty feet away. That woman that just collapsed in your cafe.

RICK. *(Pointing to woman in audience.)* Who, her?

INGRID. No, not her. She's pretty scary, though. The one that was just carried into your back room.

EITHER VERSION CONTINUES

RICK. You know, once a blackmailer is dead, dealing with them becomes considerably more complicated. You can't give in to them, twist their arm, or even threaten them with calling the police. Instead you're forced to figure out who killed them.

INGRID. Why on earth would you care about that? It sounds like this one merely got a taste of her own medicine - literally.

RICK. It's at least someplace to start in the search for your necklace. It's somewhat standard practice that blackmailers don't carry the item of blackmail on them. It's a sort of insurance policy so that the victim won't just ice them.

INGRID. She told me that she would bring the necklace to the Cafe Noir tonight and that I was to bring the money or she would turn the necklace over to my husband. I don't care who killed that French blackmailer, or why. I'm not paying you to find her killer, but my necklace. As soon as you have it or any more information, you can leave a message for me at the Blue Parrot on Tobago Cay. *(Sexy)* Perhaps you might come over to beach villa #7 after you close up tonight?

(SHEILA has entered and watches from the shadows.)

RICK. That would be rather late. And what about your suspecting husband?

INGRID. He'll be in business meetings by then. Midnight to dawn are his business hours.

RICK. I see neither of you believe in wasting the night with sleep.

INGRID. I have insomnia. I always have since Paris. The villa belongs to a friend of mine who sailed to Barbados for the weekend.

(She produces a key and hands it to him.)

INGRID. Please, Mr. Rick. I'll do anything to get that necklace. Do whatever you have to, whatever you want to.

(She turns to RENAULT.)

INGRID. I'll be waiting in your cab, Monsieur.

(She exits quickly. RICK discovers SHEILA has seen this. She turns to SIDNEY.)

SHEILA. Perhaps I will take you up on that offer for dinner on your yacht. Tell me, does she have a name?

SIDNEY. Certainly - Britannia. *(Sings)* Hail Hail Britannia, Britannia rules the waves.

RENAULT. *(Sings the French national anthem.)*

RICK. *(Sings)* I'm a yankee doodle dandy, Yankee doodle do or die. *(To audience.)* Anyone else care to sing their favorite verse?

RENAULT. Very funny, Mr. Rick. But the truth is that the disparity in the distribution of wealth in this world is becoming wider and wider. Elections are won not by votes, but by dollars. Here in the Grenadines, lands that were farmed for hundreds of years are being sold to foreign developers who cater to the decadence of wealth. They say we should be happy to be employed to serve their meals, make their beds and clean their toilets. But we are arrested if we walk on what had once been our beaches.

SIDNEY. In the real world, my friend, there are only two types of people. The served and the servers. I happen to be both. Most people are. I was a cab driver in London, until I overheard some businessmen talking about a real estate deal in my back seat. I decided to risk everything I had along with everything I could beg, borrow or talk someone out of. Success doesn't come to those who wait. It comes to those that act. It's true that you make your own destiny, but not by wishing or dreaming or complaining. You do it by risking, and losing and risking again and again until you get it right. And if you're lucky, you'll win before you die. *(Turning to SHEILA and caressing her cheek.)* It's risk that makes you appreciate the rewards all the more.

SHEILA. I thrive on risks.

(She offers her arm. He takes it and they exit.)

SIDNEY. *(To RICK.)* Here's looking at you, Kid.

(RICK is frozen in disbelief as he watches her exit.)

RENAULT. Imperial pig.

RICK. *(Eyes on the exit of SHEILA.)* Renault, you have a lady passenger waiting in your cab. Take her to the ferry to Tobago Cay.

(RENAULT exits. RICK walks to the radio, obviously hurt and turns it on. "As Time Goes By" plays. He lifts the wine bottle from the champagne bucket and gets ready to pour it into CLAUDETTE'S glass. He thinks better of it and takes a swig. CAIRO approaches him.)

CAIRO. I told you tonight was bad luck, but you wouldn't listen. You had to find out for yourself, the hard way. But I really don't think you have to worry about Ms. Wonderly.

RICK. Right. She's a big girl now. She can take care of herself.

CAIRO. She's just trying to make you jealous.

RICK. Is that what she was doing down on the docks last night with that French banker who's turned up dead?

CAIRO. I was down there too last night -

RICK. Well, don't take offense, Cairo, but you're not the woman I'm in love with.

CAIRO. Well, I'm glad of that. Perhaps, Mr. Rick, you could let the rest of the staff take care of the Cafe for the night and you and I might go somewhere quieter for a drink?

RICK. Why? So you can try and sell me printed matchbooks?

CAIRO. No, Mr. Rick.

(RICK holds up INGRID'S key.)

RICK. Cairo, you and I have known each other for a year now, so why do you still call me "Mr. Rick?" My name's just plain Rick.

CAIRO. I know, Just Plain Rick.

(RICK looks at CAIRO. They both smile. RICK throws the key into the champagne bucket.)

CAIRO. I'd throw that key even farther away. That woman is Ingrid Laszlo. Her husband is Victor Laszlo.

RICK. Should that mean anything to me?

CAIRO. Maybe not. But it does to me. Victor Laszlo happens to be the Caribbean's largest arms dealer. He is ruthless, dangerous and vengeful. He is also the reason I changed my face.

(RICK is shocked at CAIRO'S openness.)

RICK. Let me get this straight. The husband of this woman that wants me and wants me to find her pearls is an international weapons dealer and the same man you double-crossed a few years back and have been hiding out on this island from?

CAIRO. That was a long sentence even for you, Mr. Rick.

RICK. I was afraid if I paused I'd lose track of what I was saying.

CAIRO. Sometimes someone else's problems makes you forget about your own. Mine is a matter of life and death. You must help me.

RICK. Don't tell me, you want to buy my passport?

CAIRO. No, I already have a French one.

(CAIRO shows RICK a French passport he pulls from his jacket.)

RICK. This is Louis Ugarte's passport. The man who was killed on the Kingstown docks last night!

CAIRO. I literally stumbled across the body last night, after I finished securing the transportation for that handcuffs shipment.

RICK. *(Handing back the passport.)* What else did you liberate?

CAIRO. His wallet was already missing, otherwise, of course, I would have completed my collection. Tonight, it wasn't until Claudette was expiring that I realized who your Ingrid woman was and exactly what a precarious position I was in. I took the opportunity to make a hasty exit.

RICK. And here I thought you just didn't want to get stuck stowing the stiff.

CAIRO. I caught a lorry down to Green Street and Reins where the Epstein brothers hold shop, making improvements to recovered passports. Unfortunately, our friend Deputy Inspector

Rigfield was giving the place the once over. I beat a hasty retreat, but I fear the Deputy Inspector may have recognized me. I'd like you to find a safe place for this until I can get a new picture taken and a ticket on the next southbound cargo ship. I'm prepared to make this little gesture worth your while.

RICK. I've heard that before.

CAIRO. I know where Ingrid Laszlo's necklace is.

RICK. That's all fine and good, Cairo, except I don't care. I'm not looking out for Ingrid Laszlo. I have a lot of looking out to do for myself. And if you think I'm going to add to my troubles by hiding the stolen passport of a murdered man, you've been watching the wrong kind of movies.

CAIRO. But you're a man of ethics, Mr. Rick. A rare commodity in this day and age. You can't resist solving someone else's problem, no matter how much it might complicate your own.

(CAIRO hands the passport towards RICK - then freezes in place. RICK addresses the audience.)

RICK. Okay folks, what would you have done. It's time for another show of hands as it were. How many for concentrating on who slipped a fatal one to the departed Claudette in my cafe and steering clear of this dead Frenchman's passport and the pearls with the strings attached?

(There will be a show of hands.)

RICK. Okay. Now, How many for risking my neck by accepting Mr. Cairo's offer and hiding something that could implicate me in the murder of Louis Ugarte?

(There will be another show of hands. RENAULT enters, gun in hand.)

RENAULT. I'll take those pearls, Mr. Cairo.

(CAIRO drops the passport on the small table. Hands in air, he begins to back away as RENAULT edges towards him. RICK looks annoyed.)

RICK. That's a show stopper entrance, Renault. You have our attention, now put away the gun and let me get back to what I was doing. Now, how many for -
RENAULT. Not until I get those pearls. Ugarte was the international treasurer for the Liberte party. He had arranged financing for an initial purchase of arms. Last night, Ugarte was to deliver payment to the same supplier for ammunition, a quarter of a million francs worth.
RICK. And that supplier was Victor Laszlo.

(CAIRO walks behind a table, placing guests between him and RENAULT. RENAULT never loosens his aim on CAIRO.)

RENAULT. Exactament. But Ugarte never met Laszlo, and no money was discovered on his corpse. Guns are of little value without ammunition. Those pearls can be made into bullets.
CAIRO. *(Feigning ignorance.)* Pearls?
RICK. A unique idea, but a little costly, don't you think, Renault? Chances are the pearls would merely blow apart when fired anyway.
RENAULT. Very funny, Mr. Rick. Mrs. Laszlo would pay at least a quarter of a million to stop those pearls from being turned over to her husband. Ironic, that the money she would pay would

soon be returned to the same bank account.

RICK. Only the Liberte party would end up with their ammunition. Enough, Renault. Haven't you ever heard the saying, never pull a gun unless you're prepared to use it?

(RENAULT cocks the gun at CAIRO.)

CAIRO. Alright, alright. I said I knew where the pearls were. But I'll need some time to get them.

RICK. I know Cairo here may be a bit of a snake and certainly less than an honest individual - actually more than a bit of a snake. But what's the point in killing him? There are plenty of witnesses here, Renault, and as much as the St. Vincent police may not mourn Cairo's passing, they're still going to be determined to apprehend his killer. Is this radical cause of yours really worth becoming a hunted man, always on the run, bound to spend your last days as a shell of a human being huddled in the corner of a dark cell in St. Vincent's Prison?

(Both CAIRO and RENAULT stare at RICK, impressed by his description. RENAULT begins to lower the gun. CAIRO comes out from behind the table.)

CAIRO. Very convincing, Mr. Rick. But I'm not sure I like that part about being more than a bit of a snake.

(RENAULT quickly brings the gun up on CAIRO again.)

RENAULT. I'm afraid not convincing enough. The pearls, Mr. Cairo. I must insist. Your life, or even mine, pale when compared to the cause.

RICK. Oh, come on!   What a line of bull.   The cause of what? Of the French Liberte party taking over these puny little islands that boast more parrots than patriots?   And then what, Renault?   Which underprivileged party will come along and buy guns and ammunition from Victor Laszlo next? The newly oppressed become the next oppressors. Then they receive the pay-offs. And so it goes year after year, decade after decade. In poli-tics, nothing changes but the dirty faces and the hands the blood is on.

RENAULT. You sound like a man trying to convince your-self of something you don't truly believe, Mr. Rick. Perhaps it won't change anything. But we have to keep trying.

(CAIRO runs for the exit - RENAULT fires, hitting CAIRO, who shouts in pain, staggers and collapses. RICK rushes RENAULT. They fight for the gun, it ends up between them and goes off again. RENAULT staggers back - holding his gut. RICK has the gun. RENAULT staggers towards the back room door.)

RICK. You can't get far with a bullet in your gut. Let me call a doctor.

RENAULT. To keep me alive, so that I may spend my last days as a shell of a human being huddled in a cell in St. Vincent's Prison?

(RENAULT makes it to the doorway of the back room.)

RICK. You socialist fool.

RENAULT. Better that, than a capitalist one.

(RENAULT staggers through the doorway and dies, falling out of

sight with a loud crash. RICK dashes to CAIRO and looks at his wound. RICK gets up and walks over to the champagne bottle and puts the gun down on the table.)

RICK. You're not dead, Cairo. It's only a flesh wound. I wish I could say the same for Renault.

(CAIRO sits up as RICK takes a swig from the bottle. He offers it to CAIRO, who gets up and takes the bottle. As CAIRO drinks, RICK exits to the back room to check on RENAULT.)

CAIRO. *(Shouting toward the back room.)* It's true. You do see your life flash before your eyes. Mine wasn't very entertaining. If it were a movie, I'd probably have fallen asleep and missed the bang-up finale. There wasn't any romance, the violence wasn't well done and there wasn't a single character you could feel for.

RICK. *(Re-entering.)* I now have two stiffs in the back office. One male and one female.

CAIRO. Ah, romance at last. Thank you, Mr. Rick. If the situation had been the other way around - I'm sure I would have done nothing.

RICK. This new-found honesty of yours is beginning to become unbearable.

(RICK picks up the passport from the table and looks at it.)

RICK. The pearls, Cairo.

(CAIRO smiles, pulls the pearl necklace from his jacket and hands it to RICK.)

CAIRO. I was right, you are a sentimentalist.

RICK. I'm tired of all the pain they're causing. And what makes you think I won't turn all of it over to Deputy Inspector Rigfield?

CAIRO. Because the man hates you and the Cafe Noir.

RICK. Hate? A little strong, don't you think?

(RIGFIELD enters from the back room.)

RIGFIELD. An understatement if anything, Peeper. But tonight you've made me the happiest man on the island.

RICK. Forget it, Rigfield, I'm not marrying you. You're just not my type.

RIGFIELD. How about those two corpses in your back room?

RICK. I don't know about you, but I'm not into dead things.

RIGFIELD. Everything's a joke to you, eh, Peeper. We'll see how loud you laugh in St. Vincent's Prison.

RICK. I can explain, Rigfield. If you'll just -

(RIGFIELD swipes the French passport.)

RIGFIELD. And what's this? The passport of that Frenchy murdered on the Kingstown docks last night! Pinch me if I ain't dreaming. It's bloody Christmas.

RICK. Tell him where it came from, Cairo.

(CAIRO hesitates. RICK glares at him.)

CAIRO. You see, Deputy Inspector -

RIGFIELD. I see that I have this blasted yankee right where I want him. Oh ho - for the past year you've been making fun of me, haven't you, Peeper? Every time I do my job coming in here, the jokes on my blasted head.

RICK. The only time you come in here is when you try to close me down.

RIGFIELD. And that's my job. To close disreputable places like this one down and sweep the scum inside out to sea.

RICK. Don't you think you should concentrate on more important things-like the murders of Louis Ugarte and Claudette Ponte?

RIGFIELD. Ah, yes, the infamous Nurse Nightshade. She's bloody well the lady stiff in your back room ain't she?

(RICK reluctantly nods "yes.")

CAIRO. You might say she mixed her poisons.

(INGRID enters from the front door.)

INGRID. *(Anxious)* Mr. Rick?

(SHEILA quickly enters from the back room.)

SHEILA. *(About to reveal something important.)* Rick?

(SIDNEY enters from the front.)

SIDNEY. *(Business like.)* Mr. Archer -

(All three stop short upon seeing RIGFIELD.)

RIGFIELD. I've got a bloody good idea who killed that frog Ugarte down on the docks last night - and who slipped that black-

mailer one of her own mixings. And it'll be my proud and happy
duty to make this arrest.

(RIGFIELD pulls out handcuffs.)

    RICK. I suppose you'll round up the usual suspects?

(RIGFIELD slaps the cuffs on RICK.)

    RIGFIELD. Mr. Richard Archer, you are under arrest.
    RICK. Wait a second, flatfoot! You can't really be as dumb
as we make you out to be?

(RIGFIELD laughs and then sings "Gotcha.")

RIGFIELD.
YOU THINK YOU'RE SO DAMN SMART
YOU THINK YOU'RE MISTER COOL
YOU'RE LAUGHING AT THE LAW
YOU'RE BREAKING EVERY RULE
BUT YOU WON'T RULE THIS ROOST NO MORE
AND I WON'T BE YOUR FOOL
THE GIG IS UP
THIS TIME I've gotcha

I NEVER LIKED YOUR STYLE
YOU NEVER KNEW YOUR PLACE
I'M GONNA WIPE THAT SMILE
RIGHT OFF YOUR HANDSOME FACE
AND YOU'LL BE DOING TIME, MY FRIEND
IN A VERY TINY SPACE
YOUR GOOSE IS COOKED
LOOKS LIKE I GOTCHA
I'VE GOTCHA

GOTCHA WHERE I WANT CHA
AND I WANT CHA
LOCKED UP SAFE AWAY
I'VE GOTCHA
DEAD TO RIGHTS I'VE GOTCHA
AND I BET CHA I KNOW HOW TO MAKE YOU PAY

YOU ALWAYS WALK THE EDGE
BUT YOU NEVER TOE THE LINE
YOU PLAY IT FAST AND LOOSE
AND YOU CUT IT RATHER FINE
BUT NOW I'VE GOT THE EVIDENCE
I NEED TO MAKE YOU MINE
THE DEED IS DONE
I'VE FINALLY GOTCHA

I'VE GOTCHA
GOTCHA WHERE I WANT CHA
SO DON'T YOU THINK YOU CAN GET OFF EASILY
I'VE GOTCHA
PRAISE THE LORD I'VE GOTCHA
I DO BELIEVE YOU MUST AGREE
YOU ARE AS GUILTY AS GUILTY CAN BE
I WON'T LETCHA FORGET IT
YOU'R GONNA REGRET IT
I'VE GOTCHA AT LAST
GOTCHA ALL TO ME.
OH YEAH.

(The lights black out. Entree is served.)

Scene 3

(Music intro. Spotlight comes up on RICK.)

RICK. And that's how I ended up modeling manacles again. I still didn't believe in superstition, even though I had been handed two corpses in one night. I kept trying to ignore the saying "Bad things come in threes" as it kept popping into my head. When we got to St. Vincent's judicial headquarters, my luck seemed to change. It was a slow night, so I saw a magistrate right away. Lucky for me, the Magistrate on duty was the Honorable Samantha Koch. Sam, as everyone called her when she wasn't in court, was both the most criticized and respected magistrate in the eastern Caribbean. She was also no stranger to the Cafe Noir, nor our back room blackjack table. So it didn't take much to persuade her to move the inquiry back to here to Cafe Noir.

(Lights come up. RIGFIELD is pacing, obviously unhappy. RICK, still in handcuffs, stands by the radio. Beside him stands MAGISTRATE KOCH, reading a police file. Also present are INGRID, SHEILA, SIDNEY and CAIRO, who wears a bandage about his arm. They stand around the edges of the room.)

RICK. As a matter of fact, it was her idea in the first place. And that's how I ended up here, like this, bending your ear. Now I need your help in convincing her that I'm innocent and finding out whodunit.

(SHEILA hands KOCH a drink, then looks at RICK, about to say something. RIGFIELD speaks and SHEILA moves away.)

RIGFIELD. Of all the gin joints in all the towns in the world, she had to be a regular here.

CAIRO. Everyone comes to Rick's place, Deputy Inspector Rigfield.

JUDGE KOCH. Including our best court stenographer. *(To audience member.)* Thought you'd call in sick and take the day off, huh? *(She hands them a steno pad and a pencil.)* And stop pacing, Deputy Inspector. You're making me as dizzy as your report.

RIGFIELD. This is highly unorthodox, Your Honor. This man should be in a blasted jail cell. His fingerprints were found on the balmy glass that contained the poison which killed Claudette Ponte. His fingerprints were also found on the bloody gun that killed Renault. And the blasted passport of the murdered man Louis Ugarte was found in his possession. What bloody more do you want?

KOCH. For you to find some new exclamations, for one thing. I'm tired of all your balmy, bloody and blasteds.

RIGFIELD. Do you know how long I've worked for this moment? I've wanted it so bad I virtually became addicted to the taste.

RICK. And an addict will do anything to get his next fix.

RIGFIELD. What the bloody hell are you implying, Yank?

RICK. Just that you've ignored a room full of witnesses and

the Corpus Delicti.

RIGFIELD. Ignored 'em. I found both the corpses in your back room before you could hide them, didn't I?

KOCH. The Corpus Delicti, Deputy Inspector Rigfield, is the legal term for the body of the crime. In other words, all the elements of the crime and the circumstances in which it was committed. Your arrest of Mr. Archer has been purely based on circumstantial evidence.

RIGFIELD. Circumstantial? It wasn't just circumstance that had me come waltzing back in here through the back entrance.

RICK. And I'm sure it wasn't circumstance that had Ingrid Laszlo, Sidney Ferrari or my co-manager Sheila coming back to the Cafe Noir either.

KOCH. No?

RIGFIELD. I don't know about anyone else, and I don't bloody well care. But, one of those anonymous phone calls reported the corpse of Claudette Ponte enjoying the comforts of the back office of the Cafe Noir. *(To RICK.)* Not all your customers are willing to play accomplice, Peeper.

RICK. An anonymous phone call, dialed from the Blue Parrot, I'll bet. Or was it ship to shore?

(RICK glares at SIDNEY, who just smiles. SHEILA looks at SIDNEY, shocked.)

SHEILA. You weren't calling the Blue Parrot when you stopped to put in a call on our way to the marina!

SIDNEY. Just performing my civic duty.

RICK. Civic duty to get the cafe Noir for yourself.

SIDNEY. Perhaps I had some ulterior motive, but the fact remains Claudette Ponte is dead and you handed her the glass with the poison.

RIGFIELD. *(To KOCH.)* Ha! A fine witness, Your Honor. And as to Mr. Archer's heartless gunning down of the poor cab driver Renault in the back room -

RICK. *(Pointing to the table closest to him.)* These witnesses will verify that Renault was killed by accident, as I struggled to take the gun away from him.

CAIRO. After Renault shot me, Your Honor. A true act of heroism on Mr. Rick's behalf.

RIGFIELD. Poppycock! Crooked birds sing together!

(KOCH approaches the table.)

KOCH. Can you tell us, in your own words, the circumstances of how Renault was shot?

(They'll relate that RENAULT shot CAIRO, RICK rushed him and the gun went off in their struggle.)

KOCH. And what precipitated all this? Does anyone know why Renault shot at Mr. Cairo?

CAIRO. *(Lifting pearls from his pocket.)* For these, Your Honor. They belong to Mrs. Laszlo, I believe. I retrieved them from that person's salad *(Pointing to guest.)*

(CAIRO hands them towards INGRID, who attempts to take them - but RIGFIELD snatches them first.)

RIGFIELD. That's evidence, then. Give it here.

INGRID. Keep the pearls if you must, but allow me the locket?

(RIGFIELD opens the locket and reads it.)

RIGFIELD. "To my beloved Ingrid. You must remember this, a kiss is still a kiss, you are my urge of heart. Louis." Louis?

KOCH. Urge of heart! Ugarte?

INGRID. *(Crushed)* Very good, Your Honor, yes. If my husband finds out, you'll have another corpse on your hands.

RIGFIELD. How's that?

INGRID. Mine. He would have killed Louis too, if someone hadn't beat him to it.

RICK. How did you lose your pearls, Ingrid?

INGRID. *(Stalling)* Well, I - I don't really know. I -

SIDNEY. *(Short laugh.)* She threw them at Ugarte in the cocktail lounge at the Blue Parrot last night.

(INGRID looks shocked and is about to protest, but SIDNEY continues - directly to her.)

SIDNEY. He was sitting at my table at the time. We were discussing some business ventures and the possibility of securing some French investors. We had just opened an excellent bottle of Dom Perigon when this woman came storming up, flung a pearl necklace straight into Ugarte's face and then went parading out again.

(Everyone looks at INGRID. INGRID looks sheepish and tries to find a sympathetic face. She centers on SHEILA.)

INGRID. He had suddenly turned beastly to me. The French can be as romantic as a poet one moment and as cold as an accountant the next. I've never been very good at containing my emotions.

SHEILA. I'll bet that's true.

RICK. When did Claudette first attempt to blackmail you over your missing necklace, Ingrid?

INGRID. This morning.

SHEILA. *(Realizing what RICK is implying.)* And Claudette said she was down on the docks last night.

CAIRO. *(Catching on.)* So she could have found the pearls on the dock last night, in a similar manner in which I found that passport.

RICK. Exactly.

KOCH. A moment for clarification. Are you saying, Mr. Cairo, that you found Mr. Ugarte's passport on the docks last night?

CAIRO. Did I say that?

RIGFIELD. Your presence on the docks last night has already been established, Mr. Cairo. I saw you there. So you might as well come clean with it.

CAIRO. This is totally against my nature, but *(He looks at RICK, then turns to KOCH.)* Well, you see Your Honorable Madam Magistrate, being in the line of work I'm in -

KOCH. Which is?

CAIRO. Salvage, Madam Magistrate. I make my living by collecting and selling things others seem to have left behind.

RIGFIELD. The operative word there is "seem."

CAIRO. Nevertheless, far be it from me to perform an act of criminality. I discovered this discarded document on the docks. To my horror, only a few paces away, tucked into the shadows, lay the body of a dead man. I suspected that the passport was perhaps a clue. But knowing how some members of our beloved police department become overzealous with their arrests, I decided to bring the passport here to the Cafe Noir and ask Mr. Rick, whose advice is always greatly valued in these matters.

RIGFIELD. You don't seriously believe any of this taradiddle, your Magistrate?

CAIRO. Can the Deputy Inspector prove it otherwise?

KOCH. Point, Mr. Cairo.

RIGFIELD. By your own confession, you picked up the passport of a dead man on the docks last night. Earlier this evening, whilst I was chasing down a lead about some dealers in stolen passports, I spied you in a taxi making a quick u-turn at the first glimpse of me. I hear you're in a desperate hurry to get off these islands. A bloke needs a passport for that. And when a two-bit slime ball like yourself gets desperate for something - well I daresay you'd stop short of nothing, even murder, to get it.

KOCH. Point, Deputy Inspector.

CAIRO. Yeah? But Renault was the one desperate enough for those pearls to finance his radical Liberte party that he went right ahead and shot me. Maybe he plugged Ugarte.

KOCH. Fault, Mr. Cairo. Louis Ugarte was the new treasurer of the Liberte party. He and Renault were on the same side, shared the same philosophy, fought for the same cause.

CAIRO. Okay. So, forget that theory.

KOCH. *(To audience member with steno pad.)* Could you read back Mrs. Laszlo's answer as to when she was first blackmailed?

(They won't be able to, of course. KOCH takes the steno pad and reads it.)

KOCH. You're fired. Now, the theory presently on the court is that Claudette Ponte found the pearl necklace on the docks last night, either near or possibly on the dead body of one Louis Ugarte and decided to blackmail Mrs. Laszlo this morning. Your serve, Mr. Archer.

RICK. If what Renault said was true, Ugarte went to the docks to meet Victor Laszlo, with a quarter of a million francs stuffed in his pockets to buy ammunition with. But the body was discovered not only passportless, but penniless.

INGRID. *(Gasp)* You mean Victor could have killed my Louis!

RIGFIELD. Mr. Victor Laszlo spent the whole of last night at St. Vincent's Police Headquarters, arrested on charges of gun smuggling. He couldn't post bail until after the banks opened this morning.

KOCH. Point, Rigfield. Your serve, Deputy Inspector.

SIDNEY. But, according to Cairo, the pearls were discovered this evening hiding in a salad served from the kitchen of the Cafe Noir. Implying Mr. Archer was harboring them.

RIGFIELD. I thought it was my serve?

RICK. It seems we're playing doubles. Tell me, Ferrari, why did you come back here this evening?

SIDNEY. To make you an offer on the Cafe Noir. The same offer I made your co-manager.

RICK. I hope not exactly the same.

SHEILA. 100,000 francs, in cash. We'd both be kept on as managers.

(RICK is surprised at the latter part.)

SIDNEY. It wouldn't be the Cafe Noir without a wise-cracking Rick, *(To KOCH.)* would it, Your Honor?

KOCH. I'd rule not. But why in francs? The official currency here is the East Caribbean dollar. Where would you even get 100,000 francs in cash? There's not a bank in the Grenadines that could exchange that.

SIDNEY. From Louis Ugarte.

KOCH. Before or after he was dead?

RICK. Good serve, Sam, I mean your magistrate.

SIDNEY. The commercial development of Mustique was the venture we were working on together. The offer's still on the table. You're going to need it. Criminal defense lawyers don't come cheap on these islands - they're in so much demand.

KOCH. Fault. As the appointed examining magistrate, I have yet to make the decision whether the government of St. Vincent will pursue or drop charges against Mr. Archer. For clarification, Mr. Cairo, what is the exchange rate between francs and Caribbean dollars?

CAIRO. 2.7 dollars per franc.

SHEILA. That's over a quarter of a million dollars.

SIDNEY. And last year, the records show, you two bought this place for eighty thousand, with a nine percent seven-year mortgage. I'm making you an offer you can't refuse.

KOCH. I see you're good at playing the net, Mr. Ferrari. The ball's in your court, Mr. Archer.

RICK. I'll go along with whatever Sheila says. What did you decide?

SHEILA. Well - I -

SIDNEY. Perhaps you should ask her what she was doing down on the docks last night, in the company of Louis Ugarte?

KOCH. The game's picking up. Ms. Wonderly, as a court appointed official I must instruct you that you must tell the truth or be charged with perjury. Were you in the company of Mr. Ugarte on the docks last night prior to his death?

SHEILA. He was very much alive when I was with him.

KOCH. We'll take that for a yes. What were you doing?

SHEILA. With the combination of the fall off in tourism and the drop in crime our customers have less disposable income. As a result, we're behind in our mortgage payments. I was trying to get a loan for the Cafe Noir, using the only collateral I have.

INGRID. My Louis would never even consider such a proposition.

SHEILA. He jumped at the proposition, it was the loan he passed on. *(To FERRARI.)* But how did you know I was there at all?

SIDNEY. Claudette mentioned it earlier this evening.

KOCH. *(To audience.)* Is that true?

(Did CLAUDETTE mention seeing SHEILA with LOUIS UGARTE on the docks last night?)

Audience will answer "Yes."

KOCH. Nice save, Mr. Ferrari.

INGRID. Earlier this evening, while I was waiting in that back office for my cab to arrive, Ms. Wonderly came in and removed some cash from the safe. I noticed that inside was quite a few stacks of fresh francs. A hundred times more than any Frenchman would pay for an evening with the likes of her.

(SHEILA starts for her. INGRID pulls out a small gun, which her trembling hands aim at SHEILA. Everyone jumps back.)

INGRID. Stay away from me.

CAIRO. I guess she's right about not being very good at containing her emotions.

INGRID. *(Still threatening SHEILA.)* What did you do to my Louis last night?

SHEILA. Just teased him a little. You never deliver the goods until after payment in full.

INGRID. Did you kill him?
SHEILA. Did you?

(INGRID pauses for a moment, then starts to lower the gun.)

KOCH. Perhaps you would disarm the woman now, Deputy Inspector?

(RIGFIELD looks sheepish, but then musters up some pride and approaches INGRID.)

RIGFIELD. I'll take that weapon, Mrs. Laszlo, if you'll hand it over?

(She looks at him a moment. They are both tense. She hands him the gun. Everyone sighs with relief. KOCH smiles broadly.)

KOCH. Well, this is more like it. Much more exciting than sitting in one of those drab interrogation rooms in Kingstown. This is what criminal justice is supposed to be about. Rick - another drink. *(She notices his handcuffs.)* Sheila, rather. And get one for yourself, you can probably use it.

(SHEILA takes KOCH'S drink and refills it at the bar.)

KOCH. And get one for our Deputy Inspector Rigfield.
RIGFIELD. I must decline, Your Honor. I'm on duty.
KOCH. You're in my court now and what I say is the law. You may not like the way I do things, but I get things done and I do a damn fair job of dispensing justice. In the end that's really all

that matters, or at least it's all that should matter. You're having a drink and for God's sake loosen a couple of buttons, officer. It's stuffy enough in here.

RICK. Good show, Ingrid.

INGRID. What?

RICK. You were furious at Ugarte last night. Then you learned that Ugarte was to meet your husband down on the docks. You could have decided to beat him to it, desperate to get that necklace back.

INGRID. You can't be implying that I - ?

(SHEILA returns with two drinks.)

SHEILA. Of course he could. As good of a theory as I've heard yet.

(She gives a drink to KOCH and the other to RIGFIELD, who takes it reluctantly.)

KOCH. The stacks of Francs, Ms. Wonderly?

SHEILA. Oh, well - Two nights ago we were blessed with a visitation from a ship of French mercenaries bound for Haiti. Rick had taken the night off with a cold and I didn't want to go walking to the bank with that much cash alone. *(To RICK.)* I - I must have forgotten about it.

INGRID. Creative, I'll hand her that.

RICK. I'm not sure a quarter of a million francs would fit in our safe.

SIDNEY. I'm sure you've never been able to put it to the test.

KOCH. Perhaps it's time to put our justice system to the test.

(To audience.) As the examining magistrate, I'd like to use you folks as a test jury. I want you all to write down if you think Mr. Rick Archer is guilty or not - and if not, who you believe is responsible for the deaths of Louis Ugarte and Claudette Ponte. Maybe you can help speed the serving of just desserts.

(Dessert is served. SIDNEY tells everyone that RICK is guilty. INGRID tells everyone that SHEILA is guilty. SHEILA tells everyone that INGRID is guilty. CAIRO tells everyone that SIDNEY is guilty. KOCH and RIGFIELD collect the sleuth sheets. RICK tells everyone he is innocent and that he was dealing blackjack to a few regulars in the back room last night around the time of the murder of UGARTE.)

Scene 4

(Music intro. All characters are not paying attention. RICK is still in handcuffs. SHEILA gives him a drink.)

RICK. Sheila, why did you come back here tonight?

SHEILA. I almost didn't. Ferrari had already made his tempting offer on the way to the marina. I was sitting in that limousine of his, watching his luxury yacht bob idly on the waters in the bay as I waited for him to come back from making his telephone call. I thought to myself, this all could be yours. You could be living like this, day in and day out. And suddenly I felt cold. It's one thing to sell yourself out. Only you have to live with that and you can convince yourself that you've forgotten it. But to sell someone else out - ? Maybe I have too much of a conscience to live with that. I guess that's why I'm such a bad businesswoman.

RICK. I guess. So that's the only reason you came back?

(They look deep into each other's eyes.)

SHEILA. No.

(They slowly move closer to kiss, when RIGFIELD blows his whistle. They jump.)

RIGFIELD. Right. This inquiry will now come to order, Her Honorable Samantha Koch presiding. Madam Magistrate - ?

KOCH. Thank you, Ladies and Gentlemen, for aiding us in this investigation. It is the findings of this inquiry that Mr. Renault was shot by accident and thus charges for his homicide filed against Mr. Archer are hereby and forthwith dropped.

RIGFIELD. What about Claudette Ponte? He handed her the bloody drink!

KOCH. Deputy Inspector, in order to take a case to court one must establish motive, means and opportunity. Mr. Archer had no motive to kill Claudette Ponte.

RICK. But Ugarte's killer did. Claudette Ponte was poisoned because she undoubtedly witnessed something last night on the docks, or at least that's what Ugarte's killer was afraid of.

RIGFIELD. That still doesn't put you in the clear, Peeper. Where were you last night between midnight and two AM?

KOCH. I happen to know that Mr. Archer was dealing blackjack in his back office last night during the time in question - as I won a considerable amount.

RICK. Speaking of which, I'd appreciate a chance to win some of that back. What do you say, after we close up tonight, we play it again, Sam?

RIGFIELD. You're bloody well telling me that you're going to let this Shamus walk?

KOCH. By recommendation of this magistrate, there is no case against Mr. Richard Archer. Deputy Inspector, please release him.

RIGFIELD. In a ferret's eye I will. *(Pulling out "Cafe Noir" matchbook.)* What about this, found by the deceased? "Cafe Noir - exquisite island ambiance"

KOCH. *(Forceful)* Release him, Deputy Inspector!

(They look tensely at each other, a battle of wills.)

RICK. *(Quickly)* That's alright. I'll let myself out with the key I just bought from Mr. Cairo for twenty bucks.

(RICK starts to pull out the key, as CAIRO reacts with disappointment because he was named. RIGFIELD approaches CAIRO.)

RIGFIELD. Mr. Cairo, eh? Fess up, Cairo. Mr. Archer put in an order of these, didn't? Eh?

CAIRO. No - unfortunately not with me.

RICK. I didn't order them at all. It was the person who killed Ugarte because he changed his mind. And then poisoned Claudette because she may have seen too much. Ugarte was a French financier who had investments here. But he was swayed to the cause of the Liberte party. As the magistrate said, Rigfield, Ugarte shared the same philosophy as Renault. And Renault was clear about what that philosophy was - the expulsion of British rule and foreign investment. Ugarte had decided to put all his money into the Liberte party and their cause. So it is very unlikely that he would have shelled out 100,000 francs to buy the Cafe Noir and cater it to the foreign resort industry. *(Takes matchbook from RIGFIELD.)* You printed them up a little too early. You'll get a lot of exquisite island ambiance, in St. Vincent prison, Sidney Ferrari.

(RICK throws the matchbook at SIDNEY. SIDNEY pulls out a gun. RIGEFIELD grabs INGRID'S gun which was set down on the table, aiming it at SIDNEY. SIDNEY grabs SHEILA and holds her as a shield.)

SIDNEY. This is all very simple. I have my limo outside. We'll drive to the marina and put out to sea, and I'll drop your little Miss Wonderly off in a lifeboat before we sail out the harbor.

RICK. Today's Friday the thirteenth, remember? Don't you know it's bad luck to start a voyage on a Friday?

SIDNEY. I'm not superstitious. You had better put down that gun, Deputy Inspector. If you don't you'll regret - today and for the rest of your life.

(SYDNEY places the gun to SHEILA'S head. RIGFIELD puts the gun back on the table. RICK swipes the gun and pockets it as the scene continues.)

RICK. How much did Ugarte pull out?

SIDNEY. Not much, only around two million. But it was enough to get the other investors worried. By next week they'd all be pulling out, unless I could convince them we were actually expanding.

SHEILA. By buying the Cafe Noir.

SIDNEY. *(To SHEILA.)* It could have been a long and beautiful relationship *(To RICK.)* Now, if you'll excuse us, we need to be going.

(RIGFIELD steps forward.)

RIGFIELD. I'm afraid I can't let you do that.

(SIDNEY places the gun to SHEILA'S head.)

EVERYONE. Let him do it!

RIGFIELD. You wouldn't get far. As soon as you set foot

outside I'd call in to headquarters. They'd blockade the harbor. You'd have much better luck taking *(Pointing to audience member.)* him/her instead.

(SIDNEY looks back and forth between SHEILA and guest.)

RIGFIELD. Okay, how about - *(Starts to point to himself.)*

RICK. *(Interrupting RIGFIELD.)* Rigfield's right, about them blockading the harbor, Ferrari. But I now the smugglers way out. I may not be as much fun as Ms. Wonderly, but a lot more useful.

SIDNEY. Alright, Just plain Rick.

(SIDNEY pushes SHEILA towards RIGFIELD and grabs RICK, turns him around - placing the gun to his back and starts to pull RICK out the door backwards. RICK puts his hand in his pocket, pulls out the gun, hiding it from SYDNEY'S view.)

SIDNEY. Our limo awaits.

(They exit. RIGFIELD dashes towards the door when there is a gunshot outside. Everyone starts towards the door.)

RIGFIELD. Well, what in the blasted hell are you all standing around for? Someone call me a balmy ambulance.

RICK. *(Re-entering, gun in hand.)* You're a balmy ambulance, Rigfield.

SHELIA. *(Dashing to him.)* Oh, Rick.

RIGFIELD. And Mr. Ferrari?

RICK. Dead. I suppose you'll be happy now, copper. At last you have something to arrest me on.

*(RICK holds out his wrists. RIDGEFIELD approaches with the
    handcuffs.)*

    RIDGEFIELD. Well, I suppose I'll just have to - round up
the usual suspects.

(RIGFIELD passes RICK and heads to the door.)

    SHELIA. If ever you need one, Inspector Rigfield, I'll buy
you a drink on the house - at the Cafe Noir.

(SHELIA swoons RICK into a kiss. BLACK OUT.)

END

PROPS

NOTE: All props, costumes, and set decorations should be in black
& white or grey - giving the feel of a black and white 1940s movie.

Newspapers on tables
Handcuffs (two pairs)
two candles
Cafe Noir matchbook
Grey envelope stuffed with $100 bills
Hotel key
Liberta Party flyer
Pearl necklace
Radio
Wine bottle in bucket
French passport
3 guns
Police file
Steno pad and pencil

CASABLANCA REFERENCES

There are 32 references - which include names of the characters,
actors, director, writers, locations and direct line quotes – to the
movie Casablanca within the text of this play.

Also by
David Landau...

The Altos

Bullets for Broadway

Contempt of Court

Murder at Cafe Noir

Murderous Crossing

Noir Pointblank

www.ingramcontent.com/pod-product-compliance
Lightning Source LLC
Chambersburg PA
CBHW070642120726
47909CB00004B/1541